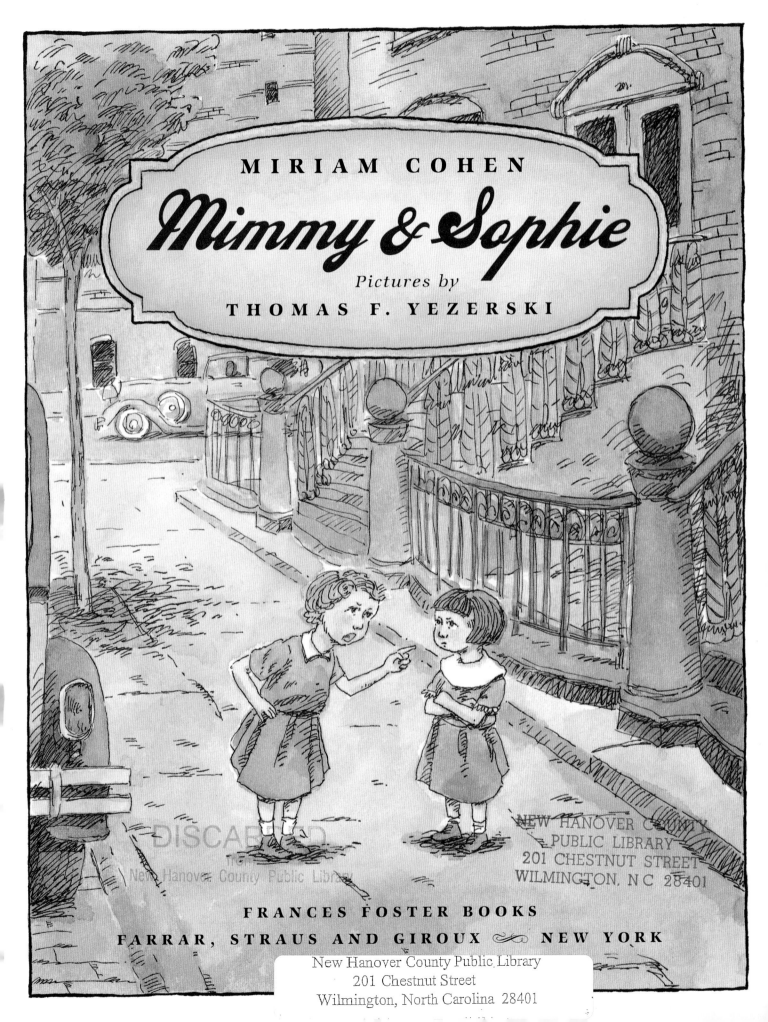

MIRIAM COHEN

# Mimmy & Sophie

Pictures by

THOMAS F. YEZERSKI

FRANCES FOSTER BOOKS

FARRAR, STRAUS AND GIROUX ❧ NEW YORK

Text copyright © 1999 by Miriam Cohen. Pictures copyright © 1999 by Thomas F. Yezerski

All rights reserved. Distributed in Canada by Douglas & McIntyre Ltd.

Printed and bound in the United States of America by Berryville Graphics

Color separations by Hong Kong Scanner Arts. Typography by Filomena Tuosto

First edition, 1999

Library of Congress Cataloging-in-Publication Data

Cohen, Miriam.

    Mimmy & Sophie / Miriam Cohen ; pictures by Thomas F. Yezerski. — 1st ed.

        p.    cm.

    Summary: Four stories about Mimmy, who is six, and her four-year-old sister Sophie; their momma, poppa, and grandparents, who emigrated from Russia; and their Brooklyn neighborhood during the Depression.

    ISBN 0-374-34988-6

    [1. Sisters—Fiction. 2. Brooklyn (New York, N.Y.)—Fiction.]  I. Yezerski, Thomas, ill. II. Title.

PZ7.C6628Mi    1998

[E]—dc21                                        97-15683

*Dedicated to Brooklyn
and to the little Mimmy I once was*

— M . C .

**To Annie, Karen, and Mary Kay**

— T . Y .

Mimmy and Sophie sat on their front steps.
"Look at this," Mimmy read. " 'Be a Lucky Winner! Just
buy a Freezy Breeze Popsicle. Look for the Lucky Stick!
Win your Dream!' "

"I'm going to be a Lucky Winner, because I'm very lucky," said Sophie. "If *I* get *my* dream," Mimmy said, "I'd drive my big shiny Oldsmobile, with tools in the trunk so I could fix it."

"I'm going to Babyland and play with all the little babies," Sophie said. "There isn't any such thing as Babyland," said Mimmy. "Every time, I tell you that." "Oh yes there is," said Sophie.

"La la la la-la la la-la,
Pop goes the weasel!"
Down the block came
the Popsicle Man's truck.

The kids on the block ran out.
"I want a Fudgy Breezer, with chocolate sprinkles!"
"Raspberry Dee-Lite, please!"
"An Orange Dreamsicle!"

"Popsicle Man, which one has the
Lucky Stick?" asked Sophie.
The Popsicle Man smiled. "Buy one
and see."
Mimmy said, "A Double Fudger,
please."
"I'll have a Cherry Dreamsicle,"
Sophie said. "Wait! No! A Raspberry
Dee-Lite. No! No! A Rainbow
Rocket." She wanted to be sure she
was picking the Lucky one.

Sophie and Mimmy
pulled the paper off their
Popsicles as fast as they
could.
"Does it say, 'Sophie
wins'?" asked Sophie.
Mimmy shook her head.
"I didn't get the Lucky
Stick. You didn't, either."
"You mean I'm not going
to go to Babyland?"

Sophie began to cry.
Mimmy said, "Now, *don't* cry!"
Sophie cried louder and louder. It was a hard job, taking care of a little sister.
Mimmy got mad at Sophie sometimes. But Sophie looked so sad with the
Popsicle dripping all over her.

"Don't cry, honey. Eat your nice Rainbow Rocket," Mimmy said.
"I don't want to!" Sophie cried and cried. "I want to go to Babyland!"
Plop! Her Rainbow Rocket fell off the stick.
"You can have mine," said Mimmy. But now her Double Fudger was just a chocolate puddle.
They could not have more nickels today. Poppa had to work very hard every day to get the nickels for Mimmy's and Sophie's Popsicles.

The Popsicle Man was watching. He reached in his truck.
"Here," he said to Mimmy and Sophie. "A Double Fudger for you, and a Rainbow Rocket for you."
"But we don't have any more money," Mimmy told him.
"Oh, that's all right," the Popsicle Man said. "These are from me, personally."

Mimmy and Sophie sat on the front steps. They ate their Popsicles very carefully.
"First, I bite some off this side. Then I do the other side to make it even," said Mimmy.
"First, *I* lick all the blue. Then I lick the pink," Sophie said.

They watched the people on their block. They looked at the sky that went so far, over all of Brooklyn.

"I can't *believe* the Popsicle Man gave us two *free* Popsicles," said Mimmy. "Boy, are we lucky!"

"I'm lucky ever since I've been born," said Sophie.

Every Sunday, Mimmy and Sophie and Momma and Poppa went to visit Gramma and Grampa. They went on the trolley car all the way down Pitkin Avenue.

"Ding, ding." The motorman pulled the cord when they were coming to a stop.

"Look, Poppa," said Mimmy. "He turns that little handle, and this whole big trolley goes right around the corner!" Mimmy was going to be a trolley driver.

122
SHOEMAKER
SHOP

"Remsen Avenue!" Mimmy and Sophie jumped down from the trolley. Gramma and Grampa were waiting in front of Grampa's shoemaker's shop.

Inside, the shoes waited to be fixed. They were tired and bumpy, like their owners' feet, but Grampa could make them shiny and new again.

"Do the belt, Grampa!" Mimmy loved to watch the wide leather belt that hummed and shook while Grampa smoothed the shoe sole.

Sophie played with the shoes. She walked them up and down so it looked as if they were talking to each other. A big man's shoe said, "My heel hurts."
An old slipper said, "You're going to feel better right away. Grampa will fix you."

Then they went in the back of the store, where Gramma and Grampa lived in a cozy apartment.

Gramma put a big pot on the table. She had brought that pot all the way from Russia.

Everybody loved Gramma's potatoes and meat and carrots in brown gravy. Mimmy and Sophie would rather have a baloney sandwich, but they would never say that.

The grownups talked and talked. They talked about the bad things that happened to their little town in Russia.

"Oy vey," said Gramma, wiping her eyes. Grampa blew his nose very loud. It was sad and dark in Russia. Gramma and Grampa were glad to live in America!

Then they had more cups of tea.

"Is it time?" Sophie whispered to Mimmy.

"Shhh. Not yet." Gramma gave Grampa a little poke.

"What? Oh." Grampa put his hand in his vest pocket. He gave Mimmy and Sophie each a nickel.

Skip, skip, skip. Mimmy and Sophie skipped as hard as they could.
"Why does Gramma cry and say, 'Oy vey'?" asked Sophie.
"Because. They were mean to Gramma and Grampa in Russia," Mimmy said.
It was getting dark on Remsen Avenue. But in one bright store window
Mimmy and Sophie knew they would see something wonderful.

Sponge cakes were
marching as if they were
in a little show. Each one
had a white cardboard
crown, with whipped
cream and a cherry on
top.
"Two charlotte russes,
please," said Mimmy.
Then they hurried back
to Grampa's.

"Look, Gramma, I'm eating a king's hat," said Sophie.
"She means a crown," Mimmy said.
"Do you know why they call it a charlotte russe?" said Grampa. "It's because they have that cake in Russia."

And Gramma told them, "The big king in Russia, the Tsar, he ate them every day. As many as he wanted—five, six, a dozen, even."
"Is that all he ate?" asked Mimmy.
"Well," Gramma said, "he ate a couple of ducks and chickens, too."
"Did he let you have some of his charlotte russe?" Sophie said.
Grampa shook his head. "Not one crumb. We didn't taste such a cake till we came here to America."
"Here, Grampa, take a bite," said Mimmy.
"You can have a bite of mine, Gramma," said Sophie.

It was really dark in Brooklyn now. They had to go home on the trolley. Mimmy and Sophie ran to get a window seat. "Goodbye, Gramma and Grampa!" They waved till the trolley went around the corner.

Mimmy watched the cars going by. "Ford, Chevrolet, Buick . . ." Sophie leaned back in the seat and kicked her legs. She was thinking.

When she got home, she took her crayons and made a picture of Gramma and Grampa. Mimmy did the words.

The next week, Grampa took a hammer and nails. He put the picture up on the wall in his shop right next to President Roosevelt. And he told all his customers, "Sophie and Mimmy, my granddaughters, made that."

Mimmy's friend Frances had a new friend. They were skating around the block, and they said Mimmy couldn't come. Mimmy sat on the steps watching them go by.

Sophie was telling her dollies a story: "So the wolf said to the piggies, 'If you will be my friends, I won't be bad to you *anymore*—'"

"That's *not* what the wolf said to the three little pigs!" Mimmy told her. "You're such a dumb bunny! And why do you always have to be where I am? Can't you go somewhere else?"
"Where?" asked Sophie.
Mimmy got up. "And *don't* follow me! You're always following me. And you're always listening when I'm trying to talk to my friends.

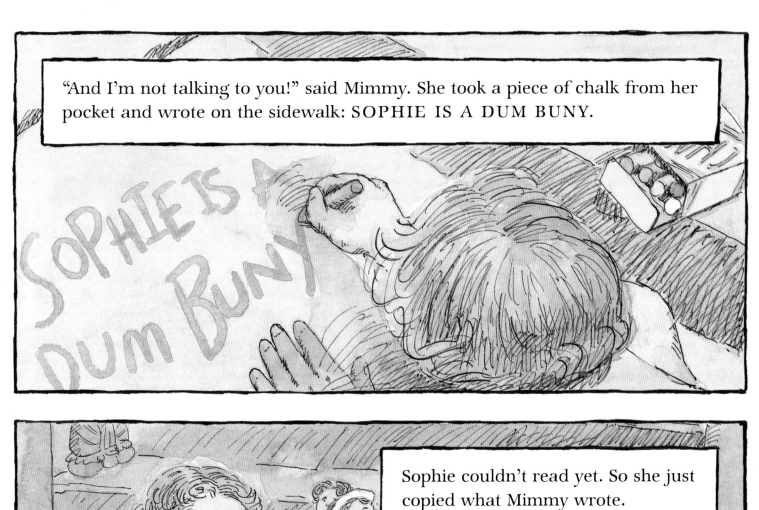

"And I'm not talking to you!" said Mimmy. She took a piece of chalk from her pocket and wrote on the sidewalk: SOPHIE IS A DUM BUNY.

Sophie couldn't read yet. So she just copied what Mimmy wrote.
"See?! You always do what I do!" cried Mimmy. "And it's supposed to say, '*Mimmy* is a dumb bunny.'"

"How do you write 'Mimmy'?" asked Sophie.

"M-I-M-M-Y," said Mimmy. Then she cried, "Don't talk to me!"

"I wasn't, I was just—"

"I'm not talking to you!" said Mimmy. And she wrote more things about Sophie on the sidewalk.

"What does it say?" asked Sophie.

Mimmy told her.

"Oh," said Sophie. Then she said, "Soon I'll be five."

Momma put her head out the window. "You aren't fighting, are you, Mimmy? You be nice to your little sister."

Mimmy shouted, "Momma, she's bothering me!" But Momma had already closed the window.

Frances and her friend skated by, holding hands. Sophie was playing with her dollies. She said, "Mimmy—" "Be quiet! Don't talk to me!"

Sophie didn't say anything for a *long* time. Mimmy began making pictures on the sidewalk. Sophie did, too.

First, Mimmy did a picture of a Buick. Then she made a Chevrolet roadster.
Sophie did a little girl. "Look at this," said Mimmy. "This car has a special speed pump. It goes forty miles an hour."

They worked hard *all* morning.

"Why are we having a fight?" asked Sophie.
"I forget," said Mimmy.
"Am I still your sister?" Sophie said.
Mimmy looked at Sophie. Then she drew this picture:

All the kids were talking about their summer vacations. Frances said, "On *our* vacation, we're going to Radio City Music Hall. We're going to see the Rockettes and everything!"

"I'm going to New Jersey to stay with my relatives," Eddy told them. "In New Jersey you can have lots of fun."

Sophie said, "We're going on vacation. We're going to Babyland."

"Don't listen to her," said Mimmy. "She just says anything."

"Where *are* you going for vacation?" Frances asked Mimmy.
"We don't know yet." But Mimmy really knew that Poppa, and Momma, and Mimmy, and Sophie couldn't have a vacation, because they didn't have enough money.
Mimmy knew why, too. It was the Depression. That meant Poppa couldn't get more money, no matter how hard he worked.

Mimmy and Sophie went inside. "Couldn't we go to stay with relatives in New Jersey for our vacation?" Sophie said to Momma and Poppa.

Poppa looked sad. Momma said, "We don't have relatives in New Jersey, Sophie. But I know something nice to do *right* now. We can go on a picnic to the Brooklyn Bridge! Mimmy, take the hard-boiled eggs out of the icebox."

Mimmy and Sophie smashed the eggs, and Momma mixed in the mayonnaise for the egg-salad sandwiches. "We'll stop at the grocery store and buy cupcakes," Momma told them.

Mimmy and Sophie loved those cupcakes from the store. There were two chocolate cupcakes in a package, and when you took a bite, there was a white, sweet cloud inside. This time they could each have their own package, instead of sharing.

"Look," Poppa said. "There's a picture of the Brooklyn Bridge on that coffee can." The Brooklyn Bridge was higher than the sky. Two giant feet were in Brooklyn, and two were in New York City. The river with teeny boats ran under it.

Riding along, Sophie told her dolly, "No, you can't have your cupcake now, honey." Mimmy asked Poppa, "If we ever got a car, which one would you pick?"

"An Oldsmobile," said Poppa.

"That's what I'd get. That's the best."

Mimmy and Sophie ran through a little tunnel and then up the big stairs to the great bridge. "Oh, look!" Mimmy cried. "You can see the whole world!"

"Is that the world?" Sophie pointed to where the sky came to the water. In between was a little smudge of land. "*That* is New Jersey," said Poppa.

Momma put newspapers down for them to sit on. Then she passed out the sandwiches. Sophie and Mimmy got to eat their cupcakes when they finished their sandwiches. "We mustn't waste food," Momma told them.

"Look at the boats way down there! Look at that big lady standing in the water!" Mimmy and Sophie said. There was so much to see!

Suddenly Sophie cried, "My dolly! Where is she?!"

"Oh, Sophie! You didn't lose her, did you?" Momma, Poppa, and Mimmy searched all over.

Sophie cried louder. Then Mimmy lifted the napkin on the picnic basket. There was Sophie's dolly!

"Did *you* put her in there?" asked Mimmy. Sophie hugged her dolly. "I forgot. I put her in there so she wouldn't get lost."

"You made us do *all* that work!" Mimmy said.

"Don't tell Momma and Poppa!" Sophie began to cry again.

But Momma and Poppa just hugged Sophie and her dolly. They didn't get mad at all. Then they all watched the night coming down over Brooklyn and the world.

The sun was a melting raspberry Popsicle on the water. The sky got more and more beautiful. It was like Momma's good blue silk dress with little stars pinned all over it.

"Oooh, a teeny airplane!" shouted Mimmy. She was so excited.

"We had the best picnic vacation. It's way better than the Radio City Music Hall Rockettes," said Mimmy.

"We saw the whole world *and* New Jersey," said Sophie. She fell asleep, and Poppa had to carry her on the way home.

"Isn't it lucky I'm big and you don't have to carry me?" Mimmy said.

And Poppa said yes, it was lucky. And Mimmy said, "We must be a *really* lucky family."